A Note to Parents and Caregivers:

Read-it! Readers are for children who are just starting on the amazing road to reading. These beautiful books support both the acquisition of reading skills and the love of books.

The PURPLE LEVEL presents basic topics and objects using high frequency words and simple language patterns.

The RED LEVEL presents familiar topics using common words and repeating sentence patterns.

The BLUE LEVEL presents new ideas using a larger vocabulary and varied sentence structure.

The YELLOW LEVEL presents more challenging ideas, a broad vocabulary, and wide variety in sentence structure.

The GREEN LEVEL presents more complex ideas, an extended vocabulary range, and expanded language structures.

The ORANGE LEVEL presents a wide range of ideas and concepts using challenging vocabulary and complex language structures.

When sharing a book with your child, read in short stretches, pausing often to talk about the pictures. Have your child turn the pages and point to the pictures and familiar words. And be sure to reread favorite stories or parts of stories.

There is no right or wrong way to share books with children. Find time to read with your child, and pass on the legacy of literacy.

Adria F. Klein, Ph.D.
Professor Emeritus
California State University
San Bernardino, California

Editor: Christianne Jones
Page Production: Tracy Davies
Creative Director: Keith Griffin
Editorial Director: Carol Jones
Managing Editor: Catherine Neitge

First American edition published in 2006 by
Picture Window Books
5115 Excelsior Boulevard
Suite 232
Minneapolis, MN 55416
877-845-8392
www.picturewindowbooks.com

Printed in the United States of America.

Library of Congress Cataloging-in-Publication Data
Law, Felicia.
Rumble meets Sylvia and Sally Swan / by Felicia Law ; illustrated by
Yoon-Mi Pak.
p. cm. — (Read-it! readers)
Summary: Two swans arrive to paint the scenery at Rumble the Dragon's Cave
Hotel and wind up choosing an unusual subject for their work.
ISBN 1-4048-1541-4 (hardcover)
[1. Swans—Fiction. 2. Artists—Fiction. 3. Hotels, motels, etc.—Fiction.
4. Dragons—Fiction.] I. Pak, Yoon-Mi, ill. II. Title. III. Series.

PZ7.L41835Rumt 2005
[E]—dc22   2005009939

Rumble Meets
Sylvia and Sally Swan

by Felicia Law
illustrated by Yoon-Mi Pak

Special thanks to our advisers for their expertise:

Adria F. Klein, Ph.D.
Professor Emeritus, California State University
San Bernardino, California

Susan Kesselring, M.A.
Literacy Educator
Rosemount–Apple Valley–Eagan (Minnesota) School District

PICTURE WINDOW BOOKS
Minneapolis, Minnesota

This is a story of a cool, young dragon named Rumble. When his grandma leaves her run-down cave to him, Rumble sets about making it into a four-star hotel. He doesn't do it all alone. He has help from a picky hotel inspector and an annoying spider named Shelby.

A pair of artistic ladies have arrived at Rumble's Cave Hotel. Sylvia and Sally Swan have brought their paints, easels, and hats. They have everything they need to make a beautiful painting. But once they are done, will anyone buy it?

"Good evening, ladies," said Rumble.
"Welcome to Rumble's Cave Hotel.
Let me help you with your luggage."

"Fourteen bags," said Shelby Spider.

"Fifteen," said Sylvia and Sally Swan.
"We have fifteen bags."

"Fourteen," said Shelby.

"Fifteen," said the Swans.

"Shhh!" Rumble whispered to Shelby.
"Don't argue with the guests."

"But they can't count," said Shelby.

"We're here to paint your scenery," said Sylvia. "The lake, the forest, and the mountains."

"That will cost a lot of money," said Shelby Spider.

"Shhh!" Rumble hissed to Shelby. "Painting the scenery is free."

"Nothing is free!" replied Shelby. "Not in this hotel!"

8

"We'll sit outside in the park," said Sally. "And, when the light is right, we'll paint."

"Right? What do you mean?" said Shelby Spider. "Our light is always right."

"Oh, no," hooted Sylvia. "We artists know all about right light and wrong light."

"Well, we only have one kind of light," said Shelby. "And it costs two pennies!"

"We will paint at dawn," said Sally, "when the light is right."

Rumble and Shelby Spider carried everything upstairs. They carried the easels, the bags with paints, the bags with brushes, the bags with canvases, AND the bags with straw hats.

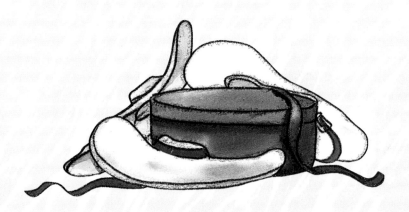

13

"We always paint in hats," said Sylvia.

"Like me?" asked Shelby Spider, putting on a hat.

"No! Like the great painter Van Gogh," said Sally.

14

"And we always wear smocks," said Sylvia.

"Like me?" said Shelby Spider.

"No! Like Van Gogh," said Sally.

Sylvia and Sally were up bright and early.

"Breakfast is served," said Rumble. "Would you like some porridge?"

"Artists don't eat porridge," they said.

But Chester the chef was worried. "They'll be hungry. I'll send them a picnic at noon," he said. "They can eat lunch in the park."

Sylvia and Sally set up their easels by
the trees.

"Too many shadows, and too much
shade," Sylvia said. "The light isn't right."

18

They set up their easels by the lake.

"Too many ripples, and too much reflection,"
Sally said. "The light isn't right."

Sylvia and Sally moved to the right ...

... and to the left.

They sat in the sun.

They sat in the shade.

But still, the light wasn't right.

At noon, Milly the maid arrived with a picnic. She spread it on a pretty cloth on the grass.

"Lunch in the park," said Sylvia. "How nice! Just like the famous painting by Monet."

"Money?" said Shelby Spider. "Lunch will cost one penny."

"What a pretty lunch," said Sally.
"It's too good to eat. Let's paint it."

The two ladies laid out their watercolors in straight rows. They squeezed paint onto their palettes and chose long, thin brushes.

Then, they started to paint.

"Incredible!" said Shelby Spider. "What a funny sight! Those swans are sitting in the most beautiful place in the world, and they're painting their lunch!"

"I agree," said Rumble. "What a waste!"

Sylvia and Sally painted all afternoon. Then, as the sun started to set, they put down their brushes. Their painting was done.

"Very impressionist! Very expressionist!" said Sally.

"It's a still life. We'll give it to you to sell, Mr. Rumble," said Sylvia.

"Thank you!" said Rumble.

"It's just a picture of a pile of food!" said Shelby Spider.

"I'm sure someone will buy it," said Rumble.

Rumble hung the painting in the lobby. Everyone gathered around to look at it.

"Hmph!" said Rumble.

"Interesting!" said Chester the chef.

"Not my taste," said Wally Warthog.

"Mmm ..." said Milly the maid.

"It must be worth a penny or two!" said Shelby Spider. "A penny for the painting!"

"No thanks!" they all said.

"We'll take it," said Sylvia and Sally Swan.

"Sold!" said Shelby Spider.

More *Read-it!* Readers

Bright pictures and fun stories help you practice your reading skills. Look for more books at your level.

Happy Birthday, Gus! by Jacklyn Williams

Happy Easter, Gus! by Jacklyn Williams

Happy Halloween, Gus! by Jacklyn Williams

Happy Thanksgiving, Gus! by Jacklyn Williams

Happy Valentine's Day, Gus! by Jacklyn Williams

Matt Goes to Mars by Carole Tremblay

Merry Christmas, Gus! by Jacklyn Williams

Rumble Meets Buddy Beaver by Felicia Law

Rumble Meets Eli Elephant by Felicia Law

Rumble Meets Keesha Kangaroo by Felicia Law

Rumble Meets Penny Panther by Felicia Law

Rumble Meets Wally Warthog by Felicia Law

Looking for a specific title or level? A complete list of *Read-it!* Readers is available on our Web site:
www.picturewindowbooks.com